NO SEDER WITHOUT YOU

No Seder Without You

PASSOVER PAST AND FUTURE

Joan Goldstein Parker

Golden Alley Press
Emmaus, Pennsylvania

A portion of the money received for every copy sold of *No Seder Without You* is going to the Yiddish Book Center (1021 West Street, Amherst, MA 01002; www.yiddishbookcenter.org)

Disclaimer: Memory greeted Imagination warmly. This book, a work of fiction, is a reflection of their meeting.

Golden Alley Press
37 South 6th Street
Emmaus, Pennsylvania 18049

www.goldenalleypress.com

Golden Alley Press books may be purchased for educational, business, or sales promotional use. For information please contact the publisher.

Printed in the United States of America

9 8 7 6 5 4 3 2 1

FIRST EDITION

Library of Congress Control Number: 2017963486

ISBN 978-0-9984429-6-9 print
ISBN 978-0-9984429-7-6 ebook

This book is dedicated to

Amy

and her children

and her children's children

because

there is no Seder without them

Contents

PART ONE

Preparing for Passover

When I was a young girl,

and the season changed from

cold winter to sunny spring,

my mother would prepare for Passover.

Before the holiday began,
I would help her clean our home,
discard our bread (every crumb),
replace the dishes and silverware,
and shop for Kosher for Passover food.

My mother and I would set the
extra-long dining table.
Three matzahs under a cloth,
a pillow on my father's chair,
a cup of wine for the Prophet Elijah,
and small bowls of salted water.

The colorful Seder plate

glowed in the center of the table.

Tiny decorated saucers nestled

in their matching-picture slots.

Unique foods filled the puzzle pieces,

symbols of our ancestors'

exodus from slavery.

Some symbols were meant to be eaten.

Others were not.

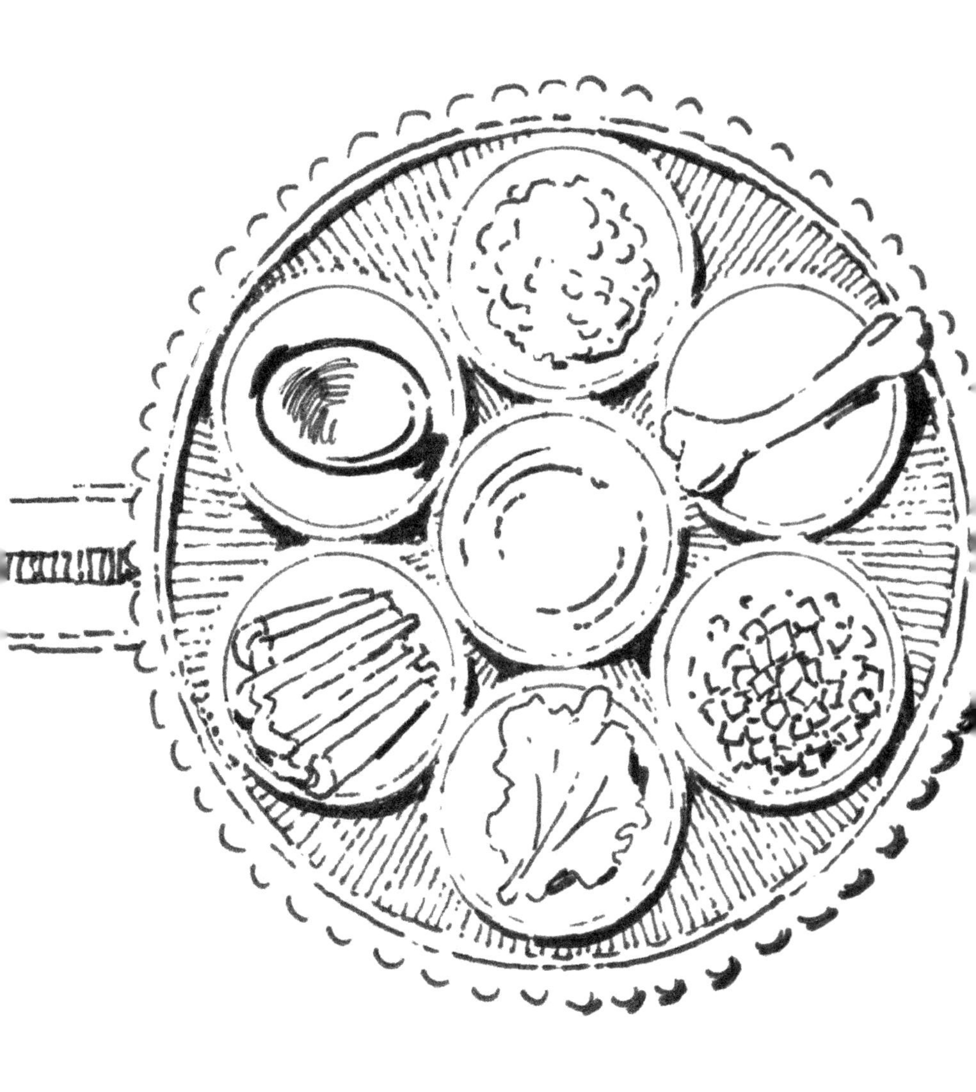

To fill the Seder plate,

we created the haroset

using two tools:

a large wooden bowl,

smooth on the outside but

deeply scarred within,

and a hand-held blade,

like a sharp-edged mirror

with a wooden handle.

No measuring cups or spoons

were allowed.

Walnuts (without their shells),
apples (without their cores),
cinnamon (ground up),
were all tossed into the bowl with
a splash of meant-for-Passover red wine.

We chopped.

We tasted.

We chopped some more.

Who knew cement could taste so sweet?

My grandmother made her homemade

horseradish more "bitter" than "herb."

When it smacked our tongues,

our eyes watered

and smoke flowed from our ears.

Every year we joked that the

secret recipe for

Grandma Miriam's maror

was being tested by

government scientists

to send rockets

into space.

Just before we lit the candles,
just before we recited the prayers,
my mother would say,
"I don't know how our family
could celebrate Passover
without your help!"

Every year,
she would tell me,
"There is no Seder without you."

PART TWO

The Seders

Family and friends,
a large group
gathered around the table.

Out loud, all together,
we read from the Haggadah.

הגדה
של
פסח

Wine stains

married finger smudges

on the worn Haggadah pages.

Their babies were tiny droplets,

crawling across the paper.

In the Haggadah,
children wonder about
the meaning of Passover.

When it was time, I recited
the Four Questions
for everyone to hear.

The Haggadah reading
answered these questions.

That's why I thought,
There is no Seder without me.

WHY IS THIS NIGHT DIFFERENT FROM ALL OTHER NIGHTS?

The Fifth Question:

How did my father hide the afikomen

without us ever seeing him?

The answer:

Magic.

(Or so we believed.)

My brother, sister, cousins, and I

would search for that broken

piece of matzah,

playing hide-and-seek

with unleavened bread.

The celebration was not complete
until the afikomen was found.

The finder was rewarded
for capturing the treasure.

There was no Seder without us.

Our Seder guest list
always included
Uncle Abe and Aunt Sara.

All year long,
they would argue.
That's how I learned the word "bicker."

But when we gathered to read the Haggadah,
everyone was on their best behavior.
Even Uncle Abe and Aunt Sara.

Our grandfather, Zeyde,
was an important Seder guest.

Like the Rabbis in the Haggadah,
he was
very old,
very wise.

I thought Zeyde was Grandpa's name.
Until I was a teenager,
when I learned that Zeyde
is Yiddish for grandfather.
My grandpa's real name
was Harold.

During Seders,

Zeyde reminded us

that Passover existed

before Haggadahs were printed,

before Haggadahs were handwritten.

Every year, Zeyde told us that

no matter what form

the Haggadah takes,

now or in the future,

there is no Seder without us.

Our Seder guest list
changed over the years.
Babies appeared.
Relatives moved away.
New friends were added.

Some changes we dreamed about
and hoped for.
Some losses we did not want
and could not undo.

We always believed
there is no Seder
without (at least some of) us.

We dipped our pinkies
in and out of cups of wine,
counting out the plagues.

When we were done,
everyone put their
wine-tipped fingers
in their mouths,
and pulled them out again.

"Ahh," we all sighed,
our special Seder sound.

The Prophet Elijah always visited our Seder
for his sip of wine.
I never saw him,
But Zeyde said he was there.

I wondered,
if Prophet Elijah
enjoyed a sip of wine
at every Seder,
by the end of the night,
did he sometimes
(like my Cousin Joshua)
have too much to drink?

The Haggadah demands
that each of us should feel as if we,
personally,
individually,
escaped from slavery
to freedom.

It is hard to see the world
through the eyes of
those who suffer.

It was hard to pretend
that we had been slaves.
But we tried.

Like the generations before us,
and the ones not yet born,
we must try to feel our ancestors' pain,
we must try to feel our ancestors' hope.

For the Jewish religion to survive,
we need to remember:
There is no Seder without us.

Now that I am an old lady,

just before Seder begins,

I gather my grandchildren around me

in a huddle,

like a football team.

Every year I say to them,

"Please remember always,

There is no Seder without you!"

PART THREE

A Passover Journal

A Passover Journal

Please use these pages to record your own Passover memories – you'll be glad you did!

Printable journal pages are available for download on our website:

http://goldenalleypress.com/no-seder-without-you/

YEAR

LOCATION

SEDER GUESTS

NOTES

YEAR

LOCATION

SEDER GUESTS

NOTES

YEAR

LOCATION

SEDER GUESTS

NOTES

YEAR

LOCATION

SEDER GUESTS

NOTES

YEAR

LOCATION

SEDER GUESTS

NOTES

Hurray Haroset!

(or, a *bisl** more about Haroset)

We know people who eat matzah, including matzah brei, all year long. Gefilte fish with horseradish, chicken soup with matzah balls, and red wine appear at several Jewish holiday tables. But haroset is a truly unique Seder food, even if it is not as famous as unleavened bread.

Haroset represents the mortar that the Israelite slaves made to build Pharaoh's cities. Mortar is that white/gray mixture that holds stones or bricks together – like the middle part of sandwich cookies. Without this filling, there are no buildings.

Since the word "recipe" usually means to combine an exact amount of ingredients, haroset is the ultimate "un-recipe." Where we come from, the requirements for haroset are: apples, walnuts, cinnamon, and Kosher for Passover sweet red wine. Among our family and friends, haroset creators are as important as its contents: often, at least one child and one adult have their hands in preparing haroset.

In our kitchens, haroset has always been made by the "chop, taste, add more (apples or walnuts or cinnamon or wine), chop again, taste again" method. These days, we buy pre-baked matzah, but we still create haroset for our Seders.

Even though we do not permit a recipe to dictate our version of haroset, there are cookbooks with haroset recipes. We like our haroset to resemble a very chunky apple sauce, but other forms of haroset range from jelly to tiny round balls. In fact, haroset is an excellent example of a Jewish food that varies according to local crops and customs.

Instead of apples, Yemenite haroset uses dates and figs. We have heard of an Italian recipe that adds dates, oranges, and bananas to walnuts and apples. Israeli haroset may contain dried fruits (but no apples) and almonds (but no walnuts).

The most surprising recipe we have seen is the one for *Egyptian* haroset. The contents are not surprising (raisins and dates), but the concept seems strange. Think about it. Can you imagine celebrating a holiday in honor of our fleeing a country in the very same country that we fled from?

* *bisl* means "little" in Yiddish

Words

Seder – The word "seder" means "order." Our traditional Passover Seder follows a specific order of events.

Haggadah – The Haggadah is the text that guides the Seder, explains the meaning of Passover symbols, and tells the story of our escape from slavery to freedom.

The Seder Plate: This platter holds several Passover symbols, including the haroset and the maror.

Haroset: A sweet mixture, intended to represent the mortar we used when we were slaves.

Maror: Grated horseradish (a root vegetable) contributes to the sharp taste of these bitter herbs.

Combining the haroset with the maror in a matzah "sandwich" reminds us that there is joy and sadness in the celebration of Passover, just as there is joy and sadness in life itself.

Matzah – Matzah is the food most often linked to Passover. In their rush to leave Egypt, our ancestors did not have time to allow bread dough to rise before baking. The result was matzah: an unleavened bread in the form of a unique, thin cracker that may be square or round.

Afikomen: When setting the Seder table, three matzahs are piled on top of each other on a plate, and under a cloth or napkin. During Seder, an adult will break the middle matzah and hide a piece of it – the afikomen – for the children to find later.

Types of Matzah: Today, there are many different kinds of matzah available: egg matzah; garlic and rosemary matzah; chocolate-covered matzah; organic and/or whole wheat and/or gluten-free matzah. For Seders, we use plain Kosher for Passover matzah.

Matzah Brei: Usually eaten at breakfast, matzah brei is a mixture of scrambled eggs and matzah.

NOTES

Spelling: Not all words are born into the English language. As a result, there are several ways to spell Passover-related terms. Our goal is simple: to use the same spelling of words throughout this book.

Literary License: Authors may know that the words they use are not accurate, but may choose to use them anyway (e.g., the plural of matzah is matzot; the plural of Haggadah is Haggadot; cement is not the same as mortar; etc.).

Thank You

For creating Seders filled with joy and for much more, I thank my parents, Leon and Emily Goldstein, of blessed memory. My brother, Bernard, and my sister, Fern, have spent decades making the-world-in-general and my-world-in-particular better places; I can't imagine finer role models. I am so fortunate to be part of a family that includes them, their spouses, their children, and their grandchildren. My husband, Alan, and I have added this book to our ever-growing list of "excellent adventures." I am deeply grateful for him as well as for our incomparable daughter, Amy. The benefits that I harvest due to my family's love and support began early in my life – with special thanks to my Great Aunt Bella Levy (a/k/a Mimi) – and continue to today.

With few exceptions (e.g., your spouse), you don't get to choose your family members, but you do select your friends. My sincerest thanks go to the following people who, over many years, have picked me to be their friend: Paula Algranati, Jodi Bogen, Wendy Doremus, Boris Draznin, Donna Etkins, Mollie Friedman, Jeff Goldstein, Boyd Griffin, Kate Hecht, Barbara Kaplan, Dolly Mack, Phyllis Miller, Donnica Moore, Elaine Nestel, Ina Potter, Helen Salinger, Lori Stein, and Elizabeth Uhlig. Space limitations prevent me from thanking every member of Bethlehem-Easton Hadassah individually, but I very much appreciate their warm acceptance. (And I am mortified to think that I have left out at least one friend and ask for forgiveness for having done so…)

For spiritual guidance, kind wisdom, and generous help with this project, thank you Rabbi Ron Isaacs, Rabbi Michael Singer, Rabbi Charles Kroloff, Rabbi Allen Juda, and Rabbi Manes Kogan. To Aaron Lansky, Susan Bronson, Sebastian Schulman and the staff of the Yiddish Book Center: *a sheynem dank* for all that you do.

Golden Alley Press devoted incredible amounts of time, energy, patience, and talent to this book; Michael and Nancy Sayre have been my true partners in this endeavor. With gratitude, I declare: there is No Book Without Them!

Author's Note

Inspired by my memories of Seders at the house where I grew up, this story ranges from truth to imagination.

My father's mother had 12 children (6 boys and 6 girls). She spent several Passovers at our home where she created bright red horseradish for the Seders. Other than beets, none of us knew what was in those bitter herbs. Smelling that horseradish made our eyes tear; tasting it made our tongues burn. Joking that her horseradish was being studied by NASA scientists as possible use for rocket fuel is an accurate record of one of our family's Passover rituals (and reflects the fact that space exploration was very much on our minds in mid-20th century America).

Unfortunately, both of my grandfathers died before I was born, and I have no memories of my mother's mother because she died when I was very young. In other words, there are parts of this book that are made up. And all of the names have been changed (but you know who you are, "Cousin Joshua!").

About the Author

Joan Goldstein Parker grew up in New York City, where the question, "Where are you going for Seder?" was always answered the same way: at her home, where three or four generations of extended family read the Haggadah and shared the meal together each year. Because it is so family-centric, the Passover Seder is her favorite Jewish tradition.

Joan has been in the publishing business all of her working life. After holding executive positions in several multinational firms, she founded her own literary agency. She and her husband live in Bethlehem, Pennsylvania. *No Seder Without You* is her first book.

The author welcomes comments from readers. She can be contacted via email: joan.parker@goldenalleypress.com.

CPSIA information can be obtained
at www.ICGtesting.com
Printed in the USA
BVHW01s0215240218
508805BV00019B/64/P